BENJAMIN
Gets Lost

Story by Maureen Spurgeon
Illustrations by Hildrun Covi

Longmeadow Press

Published in North America by Longmeadow Press
201 High Ridge Road, Stamford, CT 06904
English text copyright © 1988 Joshua Morris Publishing, Inc.
Copyright © 1988 Favorit-Verlag.
All rights reserved.
Printed in Singapore

Far to the north there is a country with huge stretches of forest, tall mountains and great lakes.

In some parts, it is easy to walk for days and days without seeing anyone at all. Snow always covers the mountaintops and only the Indians remember all the names which were once given to the lakes.

In the loneliest part of that country, Benjamin, the little brown bear, lost his way.

It happened like this.

One day, Benjamin was walking beside a lake with his mother and father. His light brown fur shone in the sunshine.

There were lots of sweet berries growing all around the lake, and it was not long before Mother Bear, Father Bear, and Benjamin were enjoying them.

Some of the best berries were too high for Benjamin to reach, but Mother Bear held down the branches with her big paw so that Benjamin could pick what he wanted.

Nearby the bears found a cave which they thought would make the perfect home.

There was plenty of sweet, juicy grass growing just outside the cave. Everything was so warm and cozy—just right for a comfortable nap in the sunshine whenever they wanted.

Each day Benjamin Bear became a little bolder, soon going for long walks all by himself.

Benjamin Bear's favorite walk was to a grassy meadow.

One day he met two chattering chipmunks. They told him that their names were Skip and Chip.

"See if you can tell us apart!" they teased him merrily.

But try as he might, Benjamin could not say which was Skip and which was Chip. The chipmunks laughed at him.

"You think you are such a big, brown bear!" they shouted.

"Yes!" Benjamin snapped back. "Of course I'm a big, brown bear!"

"Not as big as your father!" squeaked Chip.

"Not even as big as your mother!" squealed Skip. And he jumped on Benjamin's head and pulled his ears!

"I'll have my father get you!" growled Benjamin. "He'll soon eat you up!"

"Try to catch us first!" cried Chip.

"We're always very quick!" added Skip.

Just then the two naughty chipmunks were called home by their mother. "Leave that little bear alone, Skip and Chip," she scolded. "Get to work and start collecting nuts for winter."

Then Mother Chipmunk spoke kindly to Benjamin. She knew that little brown bears very quickly grow into big brown bears, so it was always best to have them as friends.

Benjamin Bear went on his way deeper into the forest. The tall, thick trees made everything very dark.

Instead of meadows with sweet, juicy grass, Benjamin could only find a few berries to eat.

By now, he was feeling frightened and very hungry. But he could not find his way back home on his own.

Poor Benjamin sat down on a big rock. "Mother! Father! It's me, Benjamin! I-I'm lost!"

Benjamin started to cry. Suddenly there came a rustling noise from the bushes.

Out came a spiky-looking creature.

"A-a porcupine!" gasped Benjamin, as the animal stopped to look at him.

It looked so fierce with all those sharp needles sticking out of its coat. Benjamin wondered if he should try running away, especially when the porcupine started rattling its quills, looking as if it meant to stick them into him!

"P-please, Porcupine—" pleaded Benjamin, "please d-do not hurt me with your quills!"

"Do not worry!" Porcupine answered. "I can see that a little brown bear like you would not attack me. But what are you doing in the forest all by yourself?"

When Benjamin explained how he had lost his way, Porcupine at once began leading the way back to the lake, even though by now it was the middle of the night.